The Gift of Christmas
A Treasury of Festive Stories
LITTLE TIGER PRESS
An imprint of Magi Publications
1 The Coda Centre, 189 Munster Road
London SW6 6AW
www.littletigerpress.com
This volume copyright
© Magi Publications 2007
All rights reserved
ISBN 978-1-84506-656-7
Printed in China
2 4 6 8 10 9 7 5 3 1

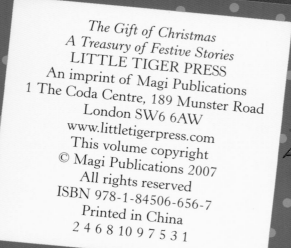

I've Seen Santa!
David Bedford
Illustrated by Tim Warnes
First published in Great Britain 2005
by Little Tiger Press,
an imprint of Magi Publications
Text copyright © David Bedford 2005
Illustrations copyright © Tim Warnes 2005

Careful, Santa!
Julie Sykes
Illustrated by Tim Warnes
First published in Great Britain 2002
by Little Tiger Press,
an imprint of Magi Publications
Text copyright © Julie Sykes 2002
Illustrations copyright © Tim Warnes 2002

Laura's Christmas Star
Klaus Baumgart
English text by Judy Waite
First published in Great Britain 2000
by Little Tiger Press,
an imprint of Magi Publications
Originally published in Germany 1998
by Baumhaus Verlag, Frankfurt
Text and illustrations copyright
© Klaus Baumgart 1998
English text copyright © Little Tiger Press 1999

Ridiculous!
Michael Coleman
Illustrated by Gwyneth Williamson
First published in Great Britain 1996
by Little Tiger Press,
an imprint of Magi Publications
Text copyright © Michael Coleman 1996
Illustrations copyright
© Gwyneth Williamson 1996

Bless You, Santa!
Julie Sykes
Illustrated by Tim Warnes
First published in Great Britain 2004
by Little Tiger Press,
an imprint of Magi Publications
Text copyright © Julie Sykes 2004
Illustrations copyright © Tim Warnes 2004

The Gift of Christmas
Christine Leeson
Illustrated by Gaby Hansen
First published in Great Britain 2000
by Little Tiger Press,
an imprint of Magi Publications
Text copyright © Christine Leeson 2000
Illustrations copyright © Gaby Hansen 2000

The Gift of Christmas

A Treasury of Festive Stories

Merry Christmas

I've Seen Santa!

David Bedford

Illustrated by
Tim Warnes

It was Christmas Eve
and Little Bear was looking
forward to seeing Santa.

"Is Santa as big as you?"
he asked Big Bear.

"Nearly," said Big Bear,
proudly.

"Oh," said Little Bear, looking worried.
"Will Santa fit down our chimney, then?"
    "Of course he will!" said Big Bear. "I'll show you."
    Big Bear went outside and climbed into
the chimney . . .

CRASH!

"See?" said Big Bear, from a cloud of soot.
"Santa will get in, no problem!"

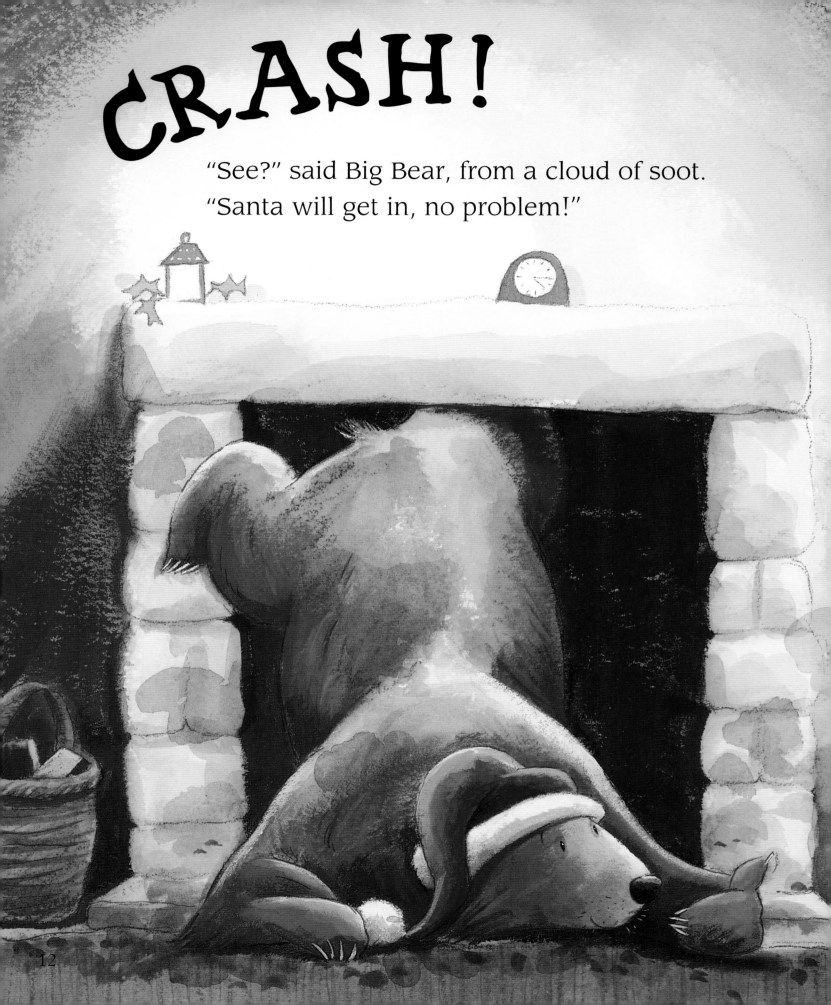

"Santa won't come if he sees this mess!"
said Mummy Bear.
"We'll help clean up," said Little Bear.

"Does Santa visit bears
all over the world?"
said Little Bear.
    "Yes," said Big Bear.
"He goes to every
house."

"Hmm," said Little Bear. "He might not have time to come here, and then I won't have any presents."
"Don't worry," said Mummy Bear. "Santa will come just as soon as you go to sleep."

For SANTA
(paws off
Big Bear)

Little Bear didn't want to go to sleep.
He wanted to see Santa. He listened to
Mummy Bear and Big Bear going to bed.
And then . . . **GLUG, GLUG, GLUG, GLUG!**

What was that noise?
Someone was downstairs!

Someone big was sitting
by the fireplace.
  "Yes!" whispered Little Bear.
"It's Santa! I've seen Santa!"
      Little Bear tiptoed up and saw . . .

. . . Big Bear!

"That's Santa's milk!" said Little Bear.
"I only wanted a sip," said Big Bear,
"before I go to sleep." He took Little
Bear's hand. "Come on, Little Bear.
Let's go to bed."

Little Bear tried to stay awake, but he soon fell into a doze.

Then a loud noise downstairs woke him up.

MUNCH! MUNCH! MUNCH! MUNCH!

Someone big was
standing by the
Christmas tree.
This time it had to be . . .

. . . Big Bear again!

"You're eating Santa's mince
pies now!" said Little Bear.
"I was hungry," said Big Bear.

"If Santa's as greedy as you,"
said Mummy Bear, coming
downstairs, "he'll be too big
and he WILL get stuck in the
chimney! Now go to bed
and go to sleep –
both of you!"

23

Little Bear went to bed, but he couldn't go to sleep. He was too worried. He woke up Big Bear to ask him a question. "What if Santa eats too many mince pies and then gets stuck in the chimney?" he whispered.

24

"Hmm," said Big Bear.
"Let's keep watch to make sure he's OK," said Little Bear. "We can hide so he won't see us."

"Shhh!" whispered Little Bear
from their hiding place.
"I can hear something!
It MUST be Santa this time!"

26

Someone was putting
presents in their stockings!
Big Bear turned on his
torch to see . . .

27

. . . Mummy Bear!

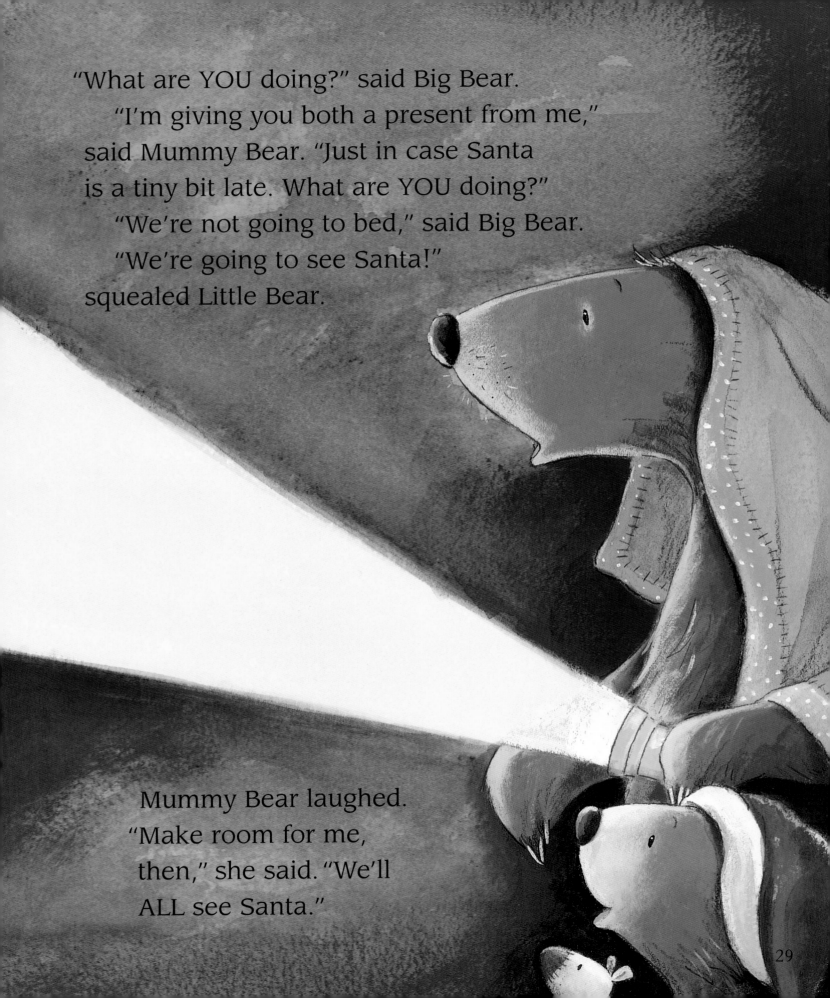

"What are YOU doing?" said Big Bear.

"I'm giving you both a present from me," said Mummy Bear. "Just in case Santa is a tiny bit late. What are YOU doing?"

"We're not going to bed," said Big Bear.

"We're going to see Santa!" squealed Little Bear.

Mummy Bear laughed. "Make room for me, then," she said. "We'll ALL see Santa."

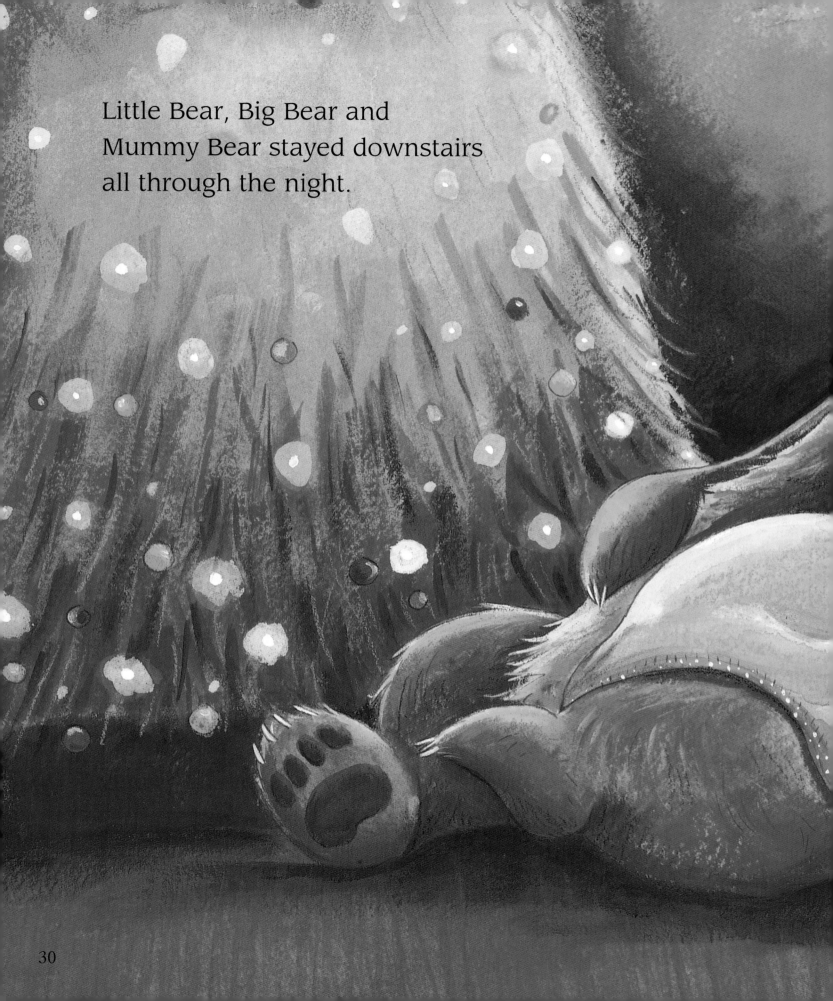

Little Bear, Big Bear and
Mummy Bear stayed downstairs
all through the night.

30

But they never did see Santa . . .

. . . even though
Santa saw them!

33

Careful, Santa!

Julie Sykes
Tim Warnes

North Pole

It was Christmas Eve, and
Santa was loading presents
on to his sleigh. Santa's little
mouse was helping too.
WHOOSH!
A gust of wind blew Santa's
beard straight in his face.
"Ho, ho, ho!" he chuckled.
"I can't see what I'm doing!"
"Careful, Santa!" warned
Santa's cat. "You mustn't
lose that sack of presents."

"That would never do!"
Santa agreed, as he carefully
stowed everything away.

Santa helped his little mouse climb aboard
the sleigh.
"Hold on tight!" he boomed. "We're off!"
It was a wild and windy night.
"Oooh my!" shouted Santa, as the sleigh
rocked this way and that. Suddenly, the sack
of presents began to move.
"Careful, Santa!" called Santa's little mouse.
"Mind that sack!"

But Santa wasn't quick enough.
The sack slid across the sleigh and toppled overboard.
"Stop!" cried Santa in alarm. "Down, Reindeer, down!
I've lost all the presents!"

The reindeer struggled
against the wind . . .

and landed as gently as they could.
"Careful, Santa!" they shouted, but it
was too late . . .
"WHOOPS!" cried Santa, landing on
his bottom.

Santa scrambled to his feet.
The presents were scattered far and
wide and he hurried to pick them up.
He didn't notice the frozen pond . . .

"*WHEEEEEE!*" cried Santa,
as he slid across the ice towards
the duckhouse.

"Careful, Santa!" quacked the ducks.
"You nearly squashed us."
"How awful," said Santa as he gathered
up the presents. "Sorry about that.
Has anyone seen my sack?"

"Here it is!" chattered a squirrel from high in a tree. Santa bravely climbed up, but before he knew it he was well and truly stuck. "Oooh, help!" he cried.

"Careful, Santa!"
called the squirrel.
"I am trying to
be careful," said Santa,
as he struggled to get free.
Very, very slowly, Santa
climbed back down again,
dropping some presents
as he went.

In the playground, a few presents were lying
under the swings. Santa put them into his
sack, then he spotted some more on the slide.

"Whooooooosh!" cried Santa, as he whizzed down the slide.
"Careful, Santa, you're going too fast!" warned Santa's cat.
"Eeek! I can't stop!" said Santa, as he zoomed towards
the snowman . . .

"Sorry, Snowman, I didn't mean to bump you," Santa said, as he dusted himself down and popped the last of the presents into his sack.

"That's it!" he boomed. "It's time to deliver
these presents. Ready, Mouse?"
But where was Mouse? Santa
couldn't see her anywhere.
"Oh dear!" he cried in alarm.
"First I lose my sack of presents,
and now I've lost my little mouse.
This will never do."

The ducks, the squirrel and Santa's cat all
crowded round.
"Don't worry, Santa!" they chattered. "She
can't have gone far. We'll help you look for her."

Everyone looked for Mouse. She wasn't in the duckhouse. She wasn't near the slide or behind the snowman.

Just then, Santa heard a familiar squeak. He shone his torch upwards . . .

and there was Mouse, hanging from a branch in a tree.
"Careful!" warned Santa. "It's far too windy to play
up there. That branch doesn't look too safe to me."

But Mouse wasn't playing. "I'm stuck," she squeaked. "Please get me down!" Quickly, Santa took off his jacket and spread it out on the ground. Everyone gathered round and held the coat like a trampoline. "Hold on tight, everyone, and don't let go!" said Santa.

"Ready, Mouse?
One, two, three . . .

JUMP!"

Mouse jumped and, with a bounce and a plop,
landed safely on Santa's coat.
"Hooray!" cheered Santa. "Thank you, everyone."

It was time to go. Santa and Mouse
hurried aboard their sleigh.
"Reindeer, up, up and away!" cried Santa.
WHOOSH! blew the wind.

"Careful, Santa," called everyone,
as the sleigh rocked this way and that.
"Look after that mouse, and HOLD
ON TIGHT TO THAT SACK!"

Laura's
Christmas Star

Klaus Baumgart

English text by Judy Waite

"Do you believe in magic?" asked Tommy, watching Laura pack her suitcase. They were going to Aunt Martha's for Christmas this year. Laura smiled. It was a quiet, secret smile.

"Sometimes," she said.

"Aunt Martha says her Christmas tree looks magical," Tommy went on. "She says it's huge and sparkly and it glitters like a zillion stars. I can't *wait* to see it."

"Are you packed?" asked Mum, coming into the room. She gave them both a hug. "It's time for bed now. Otherwise you'll both be tired and grumpy on the journey to Aunt Martha's tomorrow."

Laura closed her eyes, letting pictures of a zillion glittery stars float into her thoughts.

"Is it morning yet?" asked Tommy.

Laura opened one eye.

"We've only just gone to bed," she said. "Go back to sleep."

Laura closed her eyes again and thought of huge sparkly Christmas trees and colourful crackers.

"Is it time to get up yet?" asked Tommy.

"Not nearly," said Laura. "It's still the middle of the night."

Ten minutes passed. It seemed like ten years to Tommy.

"Is it morning *now?*" asked Tommy, nudging Laura awake.

Laura opened both her eyes. She seemed to have slept a long time. "I think it must be," she said.

Laura and Tommy jumped up, pulled on their clothes
and ran into Mum and Dad's bedroom.
"It's not time to get up," groaned Mum, waking up.
"Go back to bed!"
Laura and Tommy wandered back to their room, but they
didn't go to bed. They sat by the window, staring out at
the zillions of sparkly, glittering stars.
"Look!" cried Tommy, pointing. "That star's brighter than
the others."
Laura smiled her secret smile. The bright star was her own,
special, magic star. She had once rescued it when it had
fallen from the sky. When it was better, she had set it free.
But though it was now far away, she knew it was her friend.

Finally morning came. Laura and Tommy helped Mum and Dad pack the car. Nearby on the pavement a man was selling Christmas trees. He waved at them and shouted, "Happy Christmas!" "We're going to Aunt Martha's," Tommy shouted back. "She's got a Christmas tree that's huge and sparkly and glitters like a zillion stars."

At last they were off. The sky began to turn all grey and soft. It looked as if it was going to snow.

As they reached the country, beautiful snowflakes began to
drift down. Laura and Tommy pressed their noses against the
car window and watched them cover the earth like icing
on a Christmas cake.

Suddenly, the car began to rattle. It began to cough.

"It sounds like it's got a bad cold," said Laura.

"It sounds like it's broken down," said Mum.

Everyone got out, and Dad opened up the bonnet.
He pulled at some wires, but he didn't get the
car started.

Everyone climbed back into the car and waited for the repair man to arrive. It grew colder and colder, and everyone huddled together to keep warm. Dad tried singing Christmas songs and telling jokes, but the songs sounded flat and the jokes weren't funny.

"I'll tell you a story," said Laura. "It's about a magic Christmas star that saves everybody."

But as she started, Tommy began to cry. "There's no such thing as magic," he whispered sadly. "We'll *never* get to Aunt Martha's now. I'll never see her huge sparkly Christmas tree that glitters like a zillion stars."

By the time the repair man had
mended the car it was too late to go to Aunt Martha's.
Tommy tried not to cry as Dad drove back home and
78   they carried their suitcases into the house.

Tommy stayed sad as the daylight faded and the night crept back into the sky.

"I wish I could do something to make Tommy happy again," Laura whispered. She looked out of her bedroom, and her special star appeared. It shone down at her, as if it understood Tommy's sadness.

The man who had been selling Christmas trees had long since gone, but suddenly Laura noticed that he had left behind a little tree. It lay in the snow looking ragged and battered, and very lonely. "I'll get it for Tommy," Laura cried. "Maybe it will cheer him up."

81

Laura ran outside to where the little tree
was lying. "Come indoors with me," she
said. "You look awfully lonely out here
on your own."

Laura carried the tree into the house.

"Thanks for getting it," said Tommy sadly. "It's a nice little tree, but it's not very sparkly, is it? It's not very glittery."

Laura looked at the tree. Tommy was right.

It could never be like the magical tree Aunt Martha had promised them.

Laura went upstairs to sit by her window. At least she could tell her star how helpless she felt. It always listened to her and understood. But as she looked into the night sky, she gasped with horror. Her special star had disappeared!

Now Laura was as sad as Tommy. There wasn't much
to feel happy about now she had lost a special friend.
And maybe Tommy was right. Maybe there was no
such thing as magic after all.

Suddenly, she heard Dad calling to them.

"Laura, Tommy, come here quickly!"

Puzzled, the two children trailed downstairs.

"Look!" gasped Mum, as they all stood by the living
room door.

Laura and Tommy looked. They couldn't believe what
they were seeing.

"It's *wonderful!*" cried Tommy, turning to Laura with
shining eyes. "But how could it have happened?"

Laura smiled her quiet, secret smile.
She knew, of course. "It must be magic,"
she said.

89

Ridiculous!

Michael Coleman

Illustrated by Gwyneth Williamson

"Ho-hum," yawned Mr Tortoise. "Winter is here."
"So it is," yawned Mrs Tortoise. "Come on,
Shelley, time for bed."

"But I don't feel sleepy yet," said Shelley.

"*Ridiculous!*" cried Mr Tortoise. "All tortoises
go to sleep for the winter."
"Why?" asked Shelley.
"Because it's cold outside and there's no food."

"But I don't want to go to sleep," said Shelley.
"I want to see what winter is like!"
"*Ridiculous!*" cried Mr and Mrs Tortoise together.
"Whoever heard of a tortoise outside in winter?"

Soon
Mr Tortoise
began to snore...

and not long after
that Mrs Tortoise
began to snore...

and not long after *that*, Shelley left her warm bed of leaves, and out she went through a hole in the shed to see what winter was like.

Outside the shed, Shelley blinked.
There was snow and ice everywhere,
even on the duck pond and the hill. As
she lumbered along a duck spotted her.

"A tortoise out in winter?" quacked the duck.
"*Ridiculous!*"
"No it isn't," said Shelley.
"Oh no? Then let me see you break through
the ice to get food like *I* can. Ha-quack-ha!"
"He's right," thought Shelley. "I can't do that.
I don't have a beak."

As Shelley began to walk up the hill,
she met a dog.

"A tortoise out in winter?" barked the dog. "*Ridiculous!*"

"No it isn't," said Shelley, feeling a bit cross.

"Oh no? Then let's see you keep warm by running around like *I* can. Ha-woof-ha!"

"He's right," thought Shelley sadly. "I can't do that either."

The dog ran off after a cat, but the cat
jumped on to the branch of a tree.
She looked down at Shelley.

"A tortoise out in winter?" miaowed the cat.
"*Ridiculous!*"
"No it isn't," said Shelley, even more crossly.
"Oh no? Then let me see you run into a nice warm
  house as quickly as *I* can. Ha-miaow-ha!"
"She's right," thought Shelley, shivering with cold.
"I can't run like a dog or a cat. I'm much too slow!"

The cat raced off into her house before the dog could catch her, and Shelley trudged on up to the top of the hill, where she met a bird.

"A tortoise out in winter?" cheeped the bird.
"*Ridiculous!*"
"No it isn't," snapped Shelley.
"Oh no? Then let me see you fly off home to
   cuddle up with your family like *I* can.
    Ha-cheep-ha!"
"Of course I can't fly," thought Shelley.
"I can't even hop!"

Shelley felt cold and miserable. She remembered her
lovely warm bed and a tear trickled down her cheek.
"They're *all* right," she thought. "A tortoise out in
winter *is* ridiculous!"
Sadly she crept behind a shed where nobody could
see her crying…

and slipped on a big patch of ice!
Shelley fell over backwards and began to
slide down the hill.
Faster and faster she went...

...faster than
a *dog* could run...

faster than
a *cat*...

until suddenly she
hit a bump...

and flew into the air
like a *bird*.

Wheeee!
Down she came again and landed on the icy duck pond. She slithered towards her hole in the shed...

but it was all covered up with ice!
"Ha-quack-ha, what did I say? Where's
your beak to break the ice with?"
The duck fell about laughing.
"I don't have a beak," thought Shelley.
"But I *do* have ...

"*. . . a shell!*"
And tucking her head inside it,
Shelley smashed her way through the ice,
into the shed and home!

Mrs Tortoise woke up as she heard all the noise.
"You haven't been outside, have you, Shelley?"
she asked.
"Outside?" said Shelley, snuggling into bed.
"Whoever heard of a tortoise out in winter?"

And before you could say
"Ridiculous!"
Shelley was fast asleep.

Bless You, Santa!

Julie Sykes   Tim Warnes

It was very nearly Christmas and Santa was up early.

"Jingle bells, jingle bells," he sang cheerfully. "Breakfast first and then to work."

He filled the kettle and put on toast, but as he poured cereal into his bowl Santa's nose began to tickle.

"*Aah, aah, AAH . . .*

December 23

122

"Atishoo!"

he roared. His sneeze blew
cereal all over the place.

"Bless you, Santa," said Santa's cat, shaking cornflakes out of her tail. "That's a nasty cold."

"Dear me, no!" said Santa in alarm. "It can't be! It's nearly Christmas. I haven't got time for a cold!"

After breakfast Santa rushed to his workshop
and set to work on the unfinished toys. Merrily
he sang as he painted a robot. But Santa's sneezes
were growing larger and louder.
    "Aah, aah, AAH...

"Atishoo!"

"Bless you, Santa," squeaked Santa's little mouse, gathering the beads his sneezes had scattered.

"Bless you, Santa," said Santa's cat, chasing paper stars as they fluttered around. "You sound awful. Go and sit by the fire."

"I feel awful!" snuffled Santa. "But I can't rest yet. It's nearly Christmas and I have to finish these toys or there will be no presents for all the . . . *Aah, aah, AAH . . .*

"Atishoo!"

Santa sneezed so hard that he slipped over and landed in a stack of balls. Down the balls tumbled, bouncing off Santa and bopping around the room. They crashed into cars, they pushed over paint pots, they toppled the teddies and *ruined* the rockets.

"Atishoo!

"Just look at this terrible mess!"
wailed Santa. "I'll never be ready
in time for Christmas now!"

"Go to bed, Santa," ordered Santa's little mouse. "You're not well. Your nose is so red the reindeer could use it to guide your sleigh! We'll clear up this mess and get everything ready for Christmas."

So Santa's mouse put Santa
back to bed with a mug of hot milk
and a little something to help the cold.
Santa huddled under his duvet.
He sneezed . . .

"A t i s h o o !"

He snuffled . . .

And finally he snored.

Meanwhile, back in the workshop,
Santa's friends worked as hard as they
could. They mopped . . .

They mended . . .

They glued . . .

They snipped, they stuck and they wrapped.
Faster and faster they toiled until every
single present was finished. Then sleepily
they stumbled off to bed.

Next evening, as the sun set, the animals waited with a sleigh piled high with toys.

"But where is Santa?" asked Santa's cat. "I hope he's better!"

"Who's going to drive the sleigh and deliver all the presents?" asked the reindeer.

"Listen," said Santa's cat. "Can you hear something?"

The animals listened.

"It's Santa!" squealed Santa's little mouse. "Are you better, Santa? Can you deliver the presents?"

Santa wrinkled his nose. *"Aah, aah, AAH . . .*

"Ha ha haaa!" chuckled Santa loudly.

"Only joking! I feel much better. Bless you, everyone. You did a great job! Thanks to you all I will get these presents delivered in time for Christmas day."

Santa climbed aboard his sleigh. "Reindeer, up, up and AWAY!" he shouted.

It was a busy night as Santa flew
around the world delivering presents.

When at last Santa landed back at the
North Pole the sun was rising. But he
hadn't finished yet.

"These presents are for you," said Santa.

"Presents for us!" squeaked Santa's cat.

"Th . . . Th . . . THAA . . .

143

"Atishoo!"

Santa's cat sneezed so hard that a pile of
snow fell off the trees and buried everyone.
"Bless you!" laughed Santa. "And a
Happy Christmas to you too!"

THE GIFT OF CHRISTMAS

by CHRISTINE LEESON

Illustrated by GABY HANSEN

It was Molly Mouse's first Christmas. The sky was streaked with pink and gold, and there was a tingle in the air.

Through the window of a house something shone out and glittered in the night.
"What is it, Mum?" squeaked Molly.
"It's called a Christmas tree," said her mother.
"People cover it with shiny balls, lights and stars."
"I wish *we* had a Christmas tree," sighed Molly.
"Why not go into the woods to find one?" said her mum. "You could make it look just as pretty as that tree in the window."

Molly thought this was a wonderful idea. She called her brothers and sisters, and off they all scampered.

On the way they came to a barn and the mice rummaged through it, looking for something to add to their tree. Under a big pile of hay, Molly found a doll.
"This is like the one on the top of the Christmas tree in the window," she said. "It will be just right for our tree."

153

But the doll already had an owner.

"Grrrh!" said the old farm dog. "That's mine!"

"Don't chase us!" cried Molly. "I only thought the doll would be nice for our Christmas tree."

The old dog yawned. Sometimes, it was true, he did chase mice. But maybe because it was Christmas, or maybe because he was remembering the time when he'd played with the children by the farmhouse Christmas tree, he said the mice could borrow his toy.

155

The mice left the farmyard, carrying the doll, and reached the edge of the wood.
"Hey, I've found something else to put on our tree!" Molly shouted.
It was a golden ribbon, hanging from a branch of an oak tree. Molly scampered up the trunk, took hold of the ribbon and pulled . . .

but the ribbon belonged to a magpie.
She had taken it to line her nest.
"Please don't be cross," pleaded Molly.
"I only wanted something for our
Christmas tree."

Now usually the magpie chased mice. But maybe because it was Christmas, or maybe because she too had also been admiring the Christmas tree in the window, she let go of the other end of the ribbon and Molly took it away.

159

In the distance Molly saw some red shiny things lying on the ground. They were like the balls on the Christmas tree in the window.

"Exactly what we want!" cried Molly, running to pick one of them up. "Now we have a doll, a golden ribbon and a shiny ball!"

But the shiny balls belonged to a fox. "Those are my crab apples," he barked. "I'm burying them for the cold days ahead."

"We only thought one would look good on our Christmas tree," said Molly, trembling.

The fox sniffed. He chased mice more often than not. But maybe because it was Christmas, or maybe because he had never seen a Christmas tree before, he went back into the woods, letting Molly pick up a crab apple and carry it away.

Twilight was falling as the mice went deeper into the woods. There, in the middle of a bramble bush, they could see a lovely shining star and a dozen tiny lights glittering green and gold.

"Stars for our tree!" shouted Molly. "Let me get them." But when the little mouse reached into the bush she found not stars . . .

but a collar, belonging to an angry mother cat.
She had her kittens with her and their three pairs
of eyes shone in the dark.

"Oh dear!" gulped Molly. "I only wanted something
sparkly for our Christmas tree."
The cat pricked her ears. She always chased mice.
But maybe because it was Christmas, or maybe
because she remembered the Christmas tree in the
warm place where she'd been born, she slipped off
her old collar and let the mice take it away.

At last, in a clearing in the very
deepest part of the wood, the mice
found a large green tree. "Our
Christmas tree!" cried Molly.
On its branches they hung
the doll, the ribbon, the crab
apple and the cat's collar.

"Oh," said Molly when they had finished. "It doesn't look a bit like the tree I saw." Sadly the mice turned away and, disappointed, went all the way home to bed.

In the middle of the night Mother Mouse
woke up her little ones.
"Come with me," she whispered. "I have
something to show you."
Molly and her brothers and sisters scurried along
behind their mother, past the farm and into the woods.
Sometimes other animals hurried on ahead of them,
deep into the deepest part of the wood.

At last the mice reached the clearing
where the green tree grew. Molly stood
completely still. Her eyes grew round
and shiny.
"Oh, look at that!" she cried.

During the night the animals had all added
more decorations to the tree. The frost had
come and touched everything with glitter.
The little tree sparkled and shone and even
the stars seemed to be caught in its branches,
with the biggest and brightest star right at
the very top.

"Our tree is even better than the one in the
window," whispered Molly, happily.

And maybe because it was Christmas all
the animals sat quietly around at peace
with each other.